EFRAYIM SAV DAY

AND OTHER STORIES

BY MENUCHA FUCHS

Illustrations by Miri

Adapted by B. Goldman, B. Weinblatt and B. Zyskind

The Judaica Press, Inc. ♦ New York ♦ 2000

THE JUDAICA PRESS, INC.
718-972-6200   800-972-6201
info@judaicapress.com
visit us on the web at: www.judaicapress.com

Manufactured in the United States of America

TABLE OF CONTENTS

1. Glittering Teeth 1

2. The Library Book 11

3. Efrayim Saves The Day 21

4. The Game 29

5. The Broken Leg 37

CHAPTER ONE

GLITTERING TEETH

Shimmie glanced down at his watch for the third time. It was almost eight thirty. If Mordechai didn't hurry, they would be late for yeshiva!

"Mordechai," Shimmie called impatiently. "Mordechai, hurry up!" Shimmie was standing in the hallway of his cousin Mordechai Cohen's house. Mordechai and Shimmie were not only cousins, they were best friends. They were also in the same class in yeshiva and walked to school together each and every morning.

But this morning Mordechai was taking an extremely long time. Shimmie knew their Rebbe, Rabbi Davis, would be upset if the boys were late. Shimmie glanced at his watch and sighed.

"Mordechai," he called again. "Please hurry!"

Mordechai didn't answer. He was still in the bathroom. He had already been in there for ten minutes! Shimmie could hear a funny swish-swish sound coming from the bathroom that sounded as if Mordechai was brushing his teeth.

"Mordechai!" Shimmie called again as he knocked on the door.

Still no answer from Mordechai. Shimmie was getting angry. Now he would be in trouble with his Rebbe and it would be all Mordechai's fault.

"Mordechai, you told me that all you had to do was brush your teeth. Brushing your teeth should take a few minutes, not a few hours!" shouted Shimmie.

Mordechai still didn't answer. All Shimmie heard was the mysterious swish-swish sound.

Mordechai always took good care of his teeth. And, Shimmie admitted, it paid off. Everyone always noticed Mordechai's beautiful white teeth.

But today Mordechai was taking too long

to finish brushing. Shimmie wondered what his cousin was doing to his teeth. He looked down at his watch again: eight thirty-five.

Shimmie decided he had waited long enough! He went to the bathroom door and knocked loudly.

"Mordechai!" Shimmie called. "We're late for school and Rabbi Davis will be furious! What are you doing in there?"

There was no answer from the bathroom, but once again Shimmie heard a swish-swish sound.

"Mordechai, I don't know what you're doing or why you're making funny noises, but I'm leaving!"

Mordechai still didn't answer.

Suddenly, Shimmie got nervous. What if something had happened? What if Mordechai had slipped and bumped his head? What if...

Shimmie quickly turned the knob on the bathroom door. He pushed the door open. To his surprise, there stood Mordechai happily brushing his teeth.

"What *is* taking you so long?" asked Shimmie. "I was starting to worry."

Mordechai smiled. His mouth was filled with foam and toothpaste. He looked like he had a white mustache and beard.

Mordechai said nothing. Instead he held up two fingers.

"Are you trying to say that you'll be done

in two seconds?" Shimmie asked.

Mordechai shook his head and held up two fingers again.

"You'll be done in two minutes?" guessed Shimmie.

Mordechai shook his head again. Little white bubbles flew off his chin. Shimmie was confused. What could the two fingers mean? What was Mordechai trying to tell him?

Mordechai pointed to his toothbrush and suddenly Shimmie understood.

"You have to brush your teeth two more times!" cried Shimmie.

Mordechai smiled and nodded. Shimmie sighed. He sat down to wait.

Finally, Mordechai was ready. His teeth were sparkling. Shimmie, however was angry.

"I can't believe how late we are, Mordechai," said Shimmie. "Let's run!"

And run they did. Soon they arrived at their yeshiva. As they entered the classroom, Rabbi Davis stopped the lesson. He looked at Mordechai and Shimmie.

"Why are you boys so late?" he asked with a grim face.

Shimmie opened his mouth to explain but Mordechai spoke first. "I'm sorry, Rebbe. It's my fault. Shimmie was waiting for me to brush my teeth."

Rabbi Davis thought Mordechai was joking. "You're half an hour late because you had to brush your *teeth*?" he asked.

Mordechai nodded. He hoped that his Rebbe wouldn't punish them too badly.

"You see," Mordechai continued, "while I was brushing my teeth, I remembered that I forgot to brush last night. So I brushed again. And then I remembered that I had left my toothbrush at home on Tuesday, so I couldn't brush after lunch. So I brushed again."

The entire class was absolutely silent. Even Shimmie stared at Mordechai with disbelief.

Rabbi Davis looked at Mordechai and asked, "So you brushed three times this morning?"

"Actually," answered Mordechai, "I brushed five times. I suddenly realized that about three weeks ago—"

He never even finished his sentence. The entire class burst out laughing. Even Rabbi

Davis laughed.

After everybody finished laughing, Rabbi Davis turned to Mordechai and Shimmie and said, "I'm not going to punish you this time, boys. But next time you have to make up for all the times you couldn't brush, please do it after school. And by the way, it doesn't count to brush all at once! If you miss brushing once you *cannot* make it up another time."

"Oh, really?" Mordechai said, sounding a little disappointed.

"Really!" Rabbi Davis said and the whole class began to laugh again.

Full of relief, Shimmie and Mordechai found their seats and pulled out their Chumashim. They exchanged smiles and settled down to listen to Rabbi Davis's lesson.

CHAPTER TWO

THE LIBRARY BOOK

It was nearly midnight when Shimmie closed his book. He had spent the entire evening in his room. He hadn't left his room for dinner. He hadn't even come out when Mordechai came over to play ball.

Shimmie adored reading. He loved all

kinds of books—books that told him about places he had never seen, books that described people he had never heard of, and books that explained things he did not know. Once Shimmie started a book, everyone knew not to bother Shimmie until he finished it.

By the time Shimmie said *Shema* and turned off his

light, it was extremely late. His last thought, as he was drifting off to sleep, was about the great book he had just finished.

"Tomorrow," thought Shimmie, "I'll return the book to the school library. Mr. Ginzberg said that if I return it on time, I can take out another book! I hope he has more books by the same author!"

When Shimmie went down for breakfast the next morning, he was greeted by the usual morning craziness.

Ima had rushed out to the grocery store to pick up a container of milk. Shuli had lost her homework and was turning the house upside down to find it. Malky, who was preparing everybody's lunches, was trying to find out what everyone wanted. Four-year-old Chana was singing as she poured herself a bowl of Cheerios. When she reached her favorite part of the song, she sang so loudly that she forgot about her overflowing bowl. Leah was drawing a picture with her new markers, which she had spread all over the kitchen floor.

"Good morning, Shimmie!" called Malky. "What would you like for lunch? A tuna sandwich or a peanut butter and jelly sandwich?"

"Good morning, Malky," Shimmie replied. "Chana, you're spilling the Cheerios all over the table! Stop singing—oof!"

Shimmie slipped on one of Leah's green

markers. He fell with a loud thud. Chana stopped singing and set the box of cereal down on the table. Leah stopped drawing. Malky stopped mashing the tuna fish.

Shimmie sighed. The day was not starting out so well. Then he remembered his library book. With a smile Shimmie picked himself up off the floor and went to his room to get his book.

Shimmie walked over to his desk. He gasped in surprise. The book wasn't there! He closed his eyes and tried to remember if he had placed it somewhere else.

"Now where did that book go?" he wondered.

"Shuli," Shimmie called. "Did you see my book?"

Shuli hadn't seen the book. Leah hadn't seen the book. Neither had Malky or Chana. Shimmie searched all over his room. He peered under his bed and into his closet. He opened up all his dresser drawers and emptied out all the papers from his desk. He even looked in the trash can! But no luck! Shimmie couldn't find the book anywhere.

Malky, Shuli, Chana, and Leah felt sorry for Shimmie. They knew how important it was to him to find the book.

Malky looked for the book in the kitchen. Chana searched for it in the girls' room. Leah cleaned up her markers to see if the book was hiding under them. Shuli checked behind the couch. Shimmie looked in his backpack to see if he had already put it in there. Ima looked on top of the refrigerator and even in the dishwasher!

But nobody found the book.

Shimmie left for yeshiva upset and disappointed.

"Don't worry, Shimmie," Ima comforted him. "The book didn't walk off by itself. I'll continue looking. Don't worry, we'll find it!"

For the next few days the Levy family searched everywhere. Abba checked all the bookcases. Shimmie's sisters searched through their rooms. But the book had completely and mysteriously disappeared.

Before long it was Wednesday, the day the book was due back in the library. Shimmie didn't know what to do. What would Mr. Ginzberg say? Would he ever let Shimmie take out another book?

"I'll probably be 100 before they let me back into the library," sighed Shimmie.

"Don't worry, Shimmie," Abba told him. "I'm sure Mr. Ginzberg will understand. I'm sure the two of you will find a way to work out this problem."

During lunch, Shimmie went straight to the library to tell Mr. Ginzberg what happened. Mr. Ginzberg peered at Shimmie through his thick round glasses.

Shimmie felt so sad he almost cried! What if Mr. Ginzberg never let him take out another book from the library!

"I lost the book, Mr. Ginzberg, I'm sorry!"

Mr. Ginzberg saw that Shimmie was upset. Shimmie borrowed more books than almost anyone in the school.

"I know that you're feeling bad because you lost the book, Shimmie," said Mr. Ginzberg. "But sometimes it happens that someone loses a book."

"Will you ever let me take out another book?" asked Shimmie nervously.

Mr. Ginzberg smiled. "Of course, Shimmie! But you must make up for the book you lost. Bring me any book that's in good condition. We'll add that book to the library so other boys can take it out and read it."

Shimmie couldn't believe what Mr. Ginzberg said. He felt so happy!

"Thank you, Mr. Ginzberg! Thank you so much!" And Shimmie ran out of the library.

After school Shimmie stood before the bookcase in the family room. He was trying to decide which book he could bring to the school library.

How about the one with the short stories? he thought. No, it was Shuli's favorite book. Maybe the green one...but that was a birthday present from Ima and Abba. He couldn't give that one away!

Shimmie looked at each and every book. He couldn't decide what to do. Suddenly, Shimmie had an idea. He ran to his room and sat down at his desk. He pulled out a piece of paper and began to write. Soon Shimmie

reached for another paper, and then another. The hours passed. Shimmie still sat at his desk, writing and writing. When he finished, Shimmie found a stapler and stapled all the pages together.

The next day, during lunch, Shimmie went back to the school library.

"Mr. Ginzberg," he said proudly. "I have the perfect book for the school library!"

Shimmie handed Mr. Ginzberg his book. The librarian opened the book and began to read. He smiled and put the book away on one of the many shelves in the room.

Later that day, Shimmie's friend Nachy was in the library looking for a good book. One book held together by staples caught his eye. Nachy reached for the book and opened it to the first page. He began to read. It was about a boy named Shimmie who loved to read. One day Shimmie lost a book....

CHAPTER THREE

EFRAYIM SAVES THE DAY

Tick, tock...tick, tock. Efrayim watched the minute hand slowly move closer to the number twelve on the clock's face. School was almost over and he could hardly wait to leave. It had been a long day in yeshiva. He thought back over the terrible day.

First Efrayim had come late to class. "Efrayim, you're just in time to answer the next question in the Chumash," Rabbi Grossman said as soon as Efrayim was seated.

Efrayim turned red. He couldn't answer the question. He didn't even know the question!

He slouched down in his desk and wished he was invisible.

Later Rabbi Grossman returned the Navi tests that the boys had taken the day before. When Efrayim's name was called, he went up to get his test paper. As soon as he saw the mark on the top of his paper he felt like he had a stomach-ache. Oh no, how had he done so badly? Could this really be his test? Efrayim sighed.

At lunchtime, Efrayim's friend Meir asked, "What do you have for lunch? My mother packed a yogurt for me."

Efrayim picked up his lunch bag and peered inside. "Oh no, I took Miri's tuna sandwich. I hate tuna. I made myself a jelly sandwich but now I have to eat this, yuck!"

The day didn't improve after lunch. Efrayim's teacher called on him to read at the exact moment that Efrayim had lost the place. The teacher got angry and gave Efrayim extra homework to do.

Soon Efrayim found himself watching the clock, waiting for the long day to finally end. The clock hands seemed to take so long to move! Finally Efrayim heard the sound he was waiting for. RINNGG! The school bell rang, and suddenly the room filled with the sounds of all the students talking and packing up their bags. Efrayim breathed a sigh of relief and packed up his knapsack. He joined Meir outside  the noisy classroom. The two boys ran together for the bus.

They chose a seat near the back of the bus. All around them boys were yelling and laughing.

"Hey, do you want to come over tonight? We can play on my new computer!" shouted Meir.

Efrayim thought it over. "I'd better go straight home. The teacher gave me extra homework to do when I lost my place, remember? I'd better—hey, look at that!"

Meir turned to follow his friend's gaze. "What should I look at?"

Efrayim pointed out the window where another bus was passing by. "That boy is leaning out the window," he explained. "He is going to get hurt if he is not careful."

Meir looked. Out of a window of a bus across the street, he saw a young boy who had stuck his head completely out of the window.

"Oh, no!" said Meir. "Remember what happened to Shmuel last year? He fell out of his bus seat and broke his arm!"

Both boys watched the little blonde boy. "Someone should tell him that what he is doing is wrong," said Efrayim.

"Well, what can we do?" asked Meir.

Efrayim thought. "I know! I'll be back in a minute." Meir watched, puzzled, as Efrayim rushed to the front of the bus. Efrayim leaned over and whispered to the bus driver. Then Efrayim sat down near the bus driver. A moment later, the driver honked his horn.

Meir watched the blonde boy. At first the boy didn't realize that the bus driver was honking at him. But then he turned his head and saw the bus driver waving and beeping at him. The boy looked surprised. When he realized why the driver was honking, his face turned a bright red. He quickly ducked his head back into his bus and sat down in his seat. Efrayim walked carefully back to his seat and sat beside Meir.

"Wow Efrayim!" exclaimed Meir. "That was so smart! You probably saved his life!"

His friend shrugged. "He was acting so dangerously. How else could we warn him? I guess he doesn't know that standing on a moving bus, or sticking your head out the window of a bus is really not safe!"

A little before his bus stop, Efrayim got up to leave. The bus driver stopped him. "You know that what you did was wonderful, young man. Not many boys your age realize how dangerous playing around on a bus can be!"

Efrayim smiled, embarrassed. He remembered how Shmuel had broken his arm. Shmuel had been unable to ride his bike or play ball for a month. Having fun on a bus for a half hour was *not* worth it if you couldn't play ball for a whole month!

When Efrayim got home, Ima was waiting at the door. "How was your day?" she asked.

Efrayim smiled. "It started out really horrible, but it ended up pretty amazing!"

CHAPTER FOUR

THE GAME

Mordechai stamped his foot. "We're wasting our whole recess! We have to do something! Soon recess will be over!"

Shimmie and Yitzchok looked at Mordechai. They were standing in the back of their classroom.

"I know what I want to do," Yitzchok said. "I want to play Quick Stones."

"Me too," admitted Shimmie. "But we don't have stones to play with!"

The three boys turned to watch the rest of their classmates. All the other kids were sitting on the floor divided into small groups.

Quick Stones was the newest game in yeshiva. Each player had a set of shiny colored 'stones' they had bought. The point of the game was to win as many stones as possible.

Mordechai, Shimmie and Yitzchok were the only three boys in the class who did not own a set of stones.

"My uncle said he would buy it for me for

Chanukah," said Yitzchok.

"Well, Chanukah is months away!" cried Mordechai. "I hate watching all the other guys play Quick Stones. There must be something we could play during recess, something that is just as much fun."

"We could play ball," said Shimmie.

"No," said Yitzchok. "We always play ball!"

"Why don't we go for a walk?" suggested Mordechai.

"Boring!" called out Shimmie.

"We could sit outside and talk," said Yitzchok.

Both Shimmie and Mordechai turned to stare at their friend.

"Talk?" said Mordechai. "What are we going to talk about?"

The boys stood in silence.

"That's it," called Yitzchok. "I'm heading outside to play ball."

Mordechai and Shimmie followed

Yitzchok. They stood by the school fence and watched a group of younger boys play hide-and-seek.

"I wish my father had bought me a set of

Quick Stones," Shimmie complained.

Mordechai nodded his head. "I hate feeling left out of the fun."

Yitzchok said, "Maybe we can play Quick Stones too. Maybe someone will let us use their stones!"

Mordechai shook his head. "Everyone is already playing with their Quick Stones! Why would they let *us* borrow them?"

Shimmie glanced down at his feet. He

kicked the pebbles on the ground. There must be something he could do...some way he and his friends could have Quick Stones of their own.

Suddenly Shimmie bent down to the ground and began digging. Mordechai and Yitzchok stared at him. They wondered if he was going crazy.

Mordechai shook his head. "I always knew Shimmie was nuts!" he joked. Shimmie glanced up at his two friends. He had a strange, excited look on his face. He raised his hand happily to show them what he had found. In his palm lay three dirty pebbles.

"Very nice," exclaimed Yitzchok. "Can we go inside now?"

Shimmie laughed. "Don't you see? We can have our own Quick Stones. Real ones, too!"

Yitzchok and Mordechai finally understood. Their faces lit up. They bent down and began to search for their own

pebbles. Soon each of the boys held five bright stones in his hand. Excited, they ran into yeshiva and headed for their classroom.

"Wait till the guys see our stones!" cried Shimmie.

Mordechai stopped in his tracks.

"What's wrong, Mordechai?" asked Yitzchok.

Mordechai sighed, "I bet the boys will laugh at us when they see our stones! They bought all of their stones from a store."

The three friends were quiet for a few seconds.

Then Shimmie said, "You know what? I don't care. I'm going to play anyway. These stones are as good as the ones you can buy in a store!" And Shimmie headed into the classroom.

The rest of the class noticed Shimmie coming in. They watched with interest as he sat down and began to play.

"What are you playing with Shimmie?" called Nachy. "You don't have any Quick Stones!"

"Yes, I do," called back Shimmie, as he continued to play with his pebbles. The boys crowded around Shimmie and watched.

Mordechai and Yitzchok joined Shimmie on the floor.

"Wow," called Yossi. "Your stones are so real looking!"

"Yeah," said Menashe. "I wish I had stones like that."

"Want to trade?" asked Nachy, admiring the new stones.

Shimmie smiled and shook his head. He suddenly realized that Rabbi Davis was standing at the door. He stood and ran to his seat. All of the other boys also rushed to find their seats. Shimmie clutched his new stones in his hand.

"Sometimes," Shimmie whispered to Mordechai who was sitting next to him, "you don't need what everyone else has. I'm glad my father didn't buy me a set of Quick Stones. Now I have my very own set, from Hashem Himself!"

CHAPTER FIVE

THE BROKEN LEG

Mordechai and his cousin Shimmie were walking to school. It was a chilly, rainy morning. Shimmie was walking unusually slowly.

"Shimmie, are you okay?" asked Mordechai. "We're going to be late for class if we don't hurry. You're walking as slow as a turtle!"

Shimmie stared at the ground with a worried expression on his face. Then he looked at Mordechai and said, "I'm fine."

"Good," said Mordechai. "So let's go."

Mordechai watched his cousin. Shimmie still lagged behind him. Why was Shimmie walking so slowly in the rain? Was something wrong with his foot? Mordechai slowed down once more so that Shimmie could keep up.

The two boys finally arrived at their yeshiva and went straight to their classroom. Mordechai sat down at his desk.

Yitzchok, his classmate, was already sitting in the seat behind him.

Mordechai turned to Yitzchok. "Hey, Yitz," he whispered. "Did you notice something wrong with Shimmie's foot?"

Yitzchok stopped reviewing his notes. "No," he said looking worried. "Did he hurt himself?"

"Well, I think—" started Mordechai.

But he never finished his sentence. Rabbi Davis walked in before he could explain any further. Mordechai quickly turned around and opened his notebook. The boys began to learn.

Rabbi Davis was teaching an exciting lesson and nearly all of the boys listened carefully. Only two boys didn't pay much attention. Mordechai and Yitzchok were both worried. What was wrong with Shimmie? Would he be all right?

"No matter how many days of school

Shimmie misses," thought Mordechai, "I'll visit him every day after yeshiva is over. I'll help him make up all the classes that he misses. And I'm sure that Ima will help Aunt Bracha take good care of him."

Yitzchok, too, kept glancing at Shimmie.

Shimmie looked interested in the lesson, but Yitzchok couldn't concentrate.

"I wonder if there is anything I should do to help my friend," Yitzchok thought.

"Yossi," cried Yitzchok as soon as class was over. "Did you hear about Shimmie?"

Yossi stared at his classmate. "No," he answered. "What happened? He seemed fine in class!"

Yitzchok shook his head. "Trust me," he said. "I heard this from his cousin, Mordechai. Something's wrong with Shimmie's foot! I just hope he doesn't have to go to the hospital or anything!"

As they walked home from yeshiva, the two

boys discussed how they could help Shimmie.

The next morning, Yossi was the first to arrive in yeshiva. Nachy arrived a few minutes later.

"Nachy, did you find out what's wrong with Shimmie?" asked Yossi.

"Something's wrong with Shimmie?" asked Nachy. "I didn't hear anything about it."

Yossi explained, "Something happened to his leg. He may have to go to the hospital!"

Nachy looked sad. "I had no idea," he said. "He seemed fine yesterday."

Yitzchok joined Yossi and Nachy. "I was thinking. People usually go to the hospital if they break a bone!"

Yossi exclaimed, "So that's what happened to Shimmie. How terrible!"

Nachy nodded. "He probably won't come to school for a while."

Suddenly Mordechai came into the room.

"Hi everybody!" Mordechai shouted. "Why does everybody look so serious?"

The boys stared at Mordechai.

"You mean you don't know?" asked Yossi.

"Don't know what?" laughed Mordechai.

Nachy took a deep breath and explained, "Shimmie broke his leg."

Mordechai looked shocked. "But...how... when...?"

Yitzchok answered, "He's in the hospital. He'll probably be there for a while."

Mordechai looked sad. "But Shimmie and I just walked to school together this morning!"

The boys looked surprised.

Suddenly Shimmie ran into the room. "Hi, does anyone know what homework we were supposed to do last night?" he asked.

The boys looked confused.

"But you're in the hospital," cried Nachy.

Yossi added, "What did you do with your broken leg?"

Shimmie burst out laughing and said, "What are you talking about? Oh, I know! Mordechai was worried that something was wrong with my leg yesterday morning."

Mordechai nodded and turned to his cousin. "You walked so slowly yesterday. I thought that maybe your foot was hurting you."

Yitzchok continued, "Then I told Nachy that something was wrong with Shimmie's leg and Nachy told Yossi…"

All of the boys laughed in relief.

"It's good to know that I have such great friends," smiled Shimmie.

"What was wrong with your foot anyway?" asked Mordechai.

"Yeah," said Dovid. "It doesn't look broken!"

Shimmie laughed. "I was wearing a new pair of shoes and I didn't want to get them wet. So I tried to be careful not to step into any puddles. That's why I walked so slowly!"

The boys laughed and laughed until they noticed Rabbi Davis standing by his desk. As they returned to their seats, Nachy turned to Shimmie and asked, "Did you notice that Yitzchok's hand seems to be hurting him? I wonder if…"